Lair

Lair

Madeleine Gagnon

translated by Howard Scott

Coach House Québec Translations

Lair was first published as *Antre* in 1978
by Les Herbes rouges, Montréal,
and was reissued in 1982 by VLB Editeur in the
collection *Autographie 1. fictions.*

Antre Copyright © 1989 Madeleine Gagnon.
Lair Copyright © 1989 Howard Scott.

Published with the assistance of the Canada Council,
the Ontario Arts Council, and the Ontario Ministry
of Culture and Communications.

Cover design: Gordon Robertson.
Text design: Nelson Adams.

Printed in Canada at
The Coach House Press, Toronto

Canadian Cataloguing in Publication Data

Gagnon, Madeleine, 1938-
[Antre. English]
Lair

(Coach House Québec Translations)
Translation of: Antre.
ISBN 0-88910-374-7

I. Title. II. Title: Antre. English III. Series.

PS8563.A375A7413 1989   C843'.54   C89-094806-2
PQ3919.2.G328A7413 1989

Translator's Introduction

I was first introduced to the work of Madeleine Gagnon and other French-language women writers in a course on 'la littérature au féminin' ('writing in the feminine') at Concordia University. I felt an immediate affinity with these writings, and a fascination with their innovation in language and forms of writing. They opened my eyes to different ways of seeing women, men and how the world works. They struck chords in my heart I never knew were there.

As an undergraduate student of translation, I naturally mused on the possibility of attempting to render this writing into English. But even if I were to decide to try my hand at literary translation, I wondered if it was my place, as a man, to try to translate writing based so much on the subversion of traditional masculine discourse and on the expression and validation of women's experience. However, when it was proposed that I join three women classmates in translating feminist writers collectively, I accepted the invitation with enthusiasm. We embarked on the translation of Louky Bersianik's pivotal work *L'Euguélionne*[1] and received permission to do a collective MA thesis on the translation and theoretical problems encountered in the work. For various reasons the three women dropped out of the project, but I continued on my own, and I found myself alone as the first graduate student in women's studies at Concordia University.[2] Later when Maïr Verthuy, who had directed my thesis, suggested I translate *Antre*, I took up the challenge.

Perhaps it is presumptuous of me to attempt to translate feminist creative writing, but then any attempt to render creative writing into another language is presumptuous. To translate a creative text always means, in a sense, to make it your own, and there is the key element of women's experience in Madeleine's writing that can never be mine.

I apologize to Madeleine and the reader for every time my translation falls short, either because I am a man, or for whatever other reason. But I do not feel that being a man should exclude me from translating Madeleine's writing. I do not feel the 'feminine' in her writing is totally exterior to me, opposite to me. *Antre* also speaks to me, and of me. Madeleine reveals and explores the hidden stories of her mother and her foremothers, she seeks the sister who 'is not yet,' but she also tells of her sons. She breaks down the barriers that separate women and men, refuses the rigid dualisms of patriarchy. For her, feminism is not the battle of the sexes; it is the end of the battle of the sexes. (This is not to say, of course, that any equation can be made between what patriarchy does to women and what it does to men.) But these questions are too complex and difficult for me to even begin to deal with here. My purpose is to bring *Antre* to English-speaking readers, and I have done my best to do justice to it and to them.

Madeleine Gagnon is a key figure in the wave of French-language women writers that came to prominence in the seventies. When Elaine Marks and Isabelle de Courtivron compiled their English-language introduction to the 'new French feminisms,' Madeleine was the one North American writer they included.[3] These 'new feminist writers' attempt to break free from the built-in assumptions of language by searching for new ways of writing and thinking. They combine poetry and philosophy, theory and fiction, the personal and the political. They work words in different ways, in subversive ways, disrupting the linearity of conventional discourse, deconstructing grammar, sabotaging the symbolism of patriarchy, stripping words to their bare meanings and breaking open language to let it say what is unsaid and unsayable in the language of patriarchy. Through these linguistic transgressions, they expand cultural space to liberate territory for women's expression.

Since language is a central preoccupation of this new feminist writing, the language of the text itself becomes an important subject of the writing, and the deconstruction and transformation of vocabulary and syntax within the text becomes part of the content. In her writing, Madeleine explores language, subverting and reshaping it from the inside, sometimes creating new means of expression, sometimes going back to the roots of words, pursuing an 'archaeology' of language and, through it, of society.[4] She practises a rejuvenation of language, a recuperation of what has been silenced, a revalidation of women's words and experience.

This kind of writing presents special problems for the translator. I would like to briefly discuss two of those difficulties I encountered in *Antre*.

Grammatical gender must be handled carefully in the translation of texts where the relations between the sexes is a central concern. In French, the fact that all nouns and third-person pronouns are either feminine or masculine, and the rule that the masculine 'embraces' the feminine cause difficulties for those concerned with sexism in language. It has certainly proven an obstacle to the introduction of inclusive language. In new feminist writing, this masculine bias in the grammar is often used to advantage. The gender of nouns and pronouns becomes a tool the writer uses to comment on language and society.

In translating *Antre*, always rendering 'elles' and 'ils' as 'they' would have been a definite error. When these pronouns refer to people, their gender is usually important. I toyed with the idea of trying to distinguish two 'they's' in English, one feminine and one masculine, by capitalizing one or using some other graphic device, but rejected this idea since it was a visual manipulation of language not used in the original; it would have constituted an unwarranted disruption in the text. I opted, finally, for using the singular 'she' to translate 'elles' where the feminine gender was important; this is the mirror image of the tactic of avoiding the generic use of 'he' in English by switching to a plural, e.g. 'Doctors.... They....' instead of 'A doctor.... He....' For example, on page 27, I translated, 'carnés de haine ces enfants capotés dont *elles* ont disent-ils dévoré le coeur' by 'flesh-coloured with hate these flipped children whose hearts, they say, *she* has devoured' (my italics). 'They,' on the other hand, seemed to work for the masculine plural. In context, 'they' feels solidly masculine to me when it is not specifically feminine; it is the norm versus the specific, the marked, the Other. For example, on page 14, '... they preached logical metaphor and coherent images to me. I quenched my thirst on their nonsense at the gates of accepted madnesses and absolved murders, ...' This solution sacrifices the feminine plural, which in many instances would be more appropriate than the singular, but it preserves the gender distinction which is essential to the text.

Other central themes and key words also presented problems. Madeleine and other writers speak of 'writing the body,' saying that their way of writing proceeds from the body, that the sexual differentiation of women is also a source of their creativity and distinguishes their work from traditional patriarchal writing.

Central to this theme of 'writing the body' is the concept of 'jouissance.' 'Jouissance' and the corresponding verb 'jouir' are key words in *Antre*. In everyday writing these words are often tricky to translate into English. Their special significance in new feminist writing can make them even more difficult. Literally, 'jouissance' means 'enjoyment' or 'pleasure.' It can refer to many kinds of enjoyment, including enjoyment in the legal sense or 'enjoyment of good health.' But in the writings of Madeleine and other French-language feminist writers, 'jouissance' refers primarily to sensual pleasure, sensual pleasure covering the whole range from joy of self-discovery and self-realization, to sexual orgasm ('jouir' can mean simply 'to come').

The importance of 'jouissance' presents a special problem in translating *Antre*. While, in other contexts, the various occurrences of 'jouir' and 'jouissance' might have been translated in various ways, or even paraphrased, in *Antre* such solutions would have erased a key element of the work. To use a weaving image, a favourite one of Madeleine's, 'jouissance' is like a brightly-coloured thread running through a tapestry; if the thread changes colour, the intricate pattern of the tapestry is destroyed. I therefore felt it essential to translate 'jouissance' consistently.

I finally decided to use 'pleasure' for both the verb 'jouir' and the noun 'jouissance.' 'To pleasure' is not quite the equivalent of 'jouir' since the former is primarily transitive and the latter normally intransitive, but this presented no major problems. In fact, at one point, Madeleine makes 'jouir' transitive (... tu n'as pas droit de jouir.... D'être jouie.' – '... you have no right to pleasure.... To be pleasured.' p. 19). 'Pleasure' as a verb may seem archaic, but I feel it best conveys the flavour of the original. And I like the idea of 'pleasuring' and 'being pleasured' whether in a purely sexual, or more figurative, sense. It is the same kind of recuperation and revitalization of fossilized words and meanings, and forgotten or obscured experience that Madeleine practises.

I am solely responsible for the final version of this translation, but it was by no means a solo effort. My re-reading of *Antre* was shared with Madeleine, with my companion in life, Phyllis, and especially with fellow translator and Madeleine's long-time friend, and now my friend, Jean-Antonin Billard.

Howard Scott
May 1989

NOTES

1 (Montréal: Les Editions La Presse, 1976). An excerpt of our translation was published in *Canadian Women's Studies / Les Cahiers de la Femme*, vol. 1, no. 3, (spring / printemps 1979), pp. 71-75. Another translation of the book has been published: *The Euguélionne*, translated by Gerry Denis, Alison Hewitt, Donna Murray, Martha O'Brien (Victoria, Toronto: Press Porcépic, 1982).

2 'Louky Bersianik's *L'Euguélionne*: Problems of Translating the Critique of Language in New Québec Feminist Writing,' unpublished thesis (Concordia University, 1984).
3 'Body I,' in *New French Feminisms: An Anthology,* translated by Isabelle de Courtivron. (Amherst: The University of Massachusetts Press, 1980), pp. 179-180. Excerpt from 'Mon Corps dans l'écriture,' in *La Venue à l'écriture* (with Hélène Cixous and Annie Leclerc) (Paris: Union Générale d'Editions, 1977), pp. 63-116.
4 Another of her books, *Lueur (Glimmer)* (Montréal: VLB Editeur, 1979), is subtitled *Archaeological Novel*.

There is an egg in this dream of a book born of orgasm, I who was. Nothing showed me that all of it could be written in the feminine, however. I followed the syntax learned, as if blindly, I no longer felt a part of it, through my eyes from the inside, only. Deaf to my own cries, meaningful words came to be beyond me, howls. I knew that to transcribe them would no longer be my loss and decided never again to work those calm results of pure toil. So I sat down to wait for myself savouring your ephemeral warmth. We were two to be born and no one left to deny us, except what still inside and from far away intruded afraid between us. We were sure of it. And a lot of people had almost stayed there our passion resided in the place of their desire, of ours, of writing it without dying, from now on.

To each according to that love, so fleeting and tenuous, volcanic and so calm, in spite of everything, which deceives appearances of nothing. Those who think they understood it before me should come explain to me what I just wrote inside my order said to be my fear, I am not afraid of those words, because they contained a brief moment where in order to feel alive I had to burn myself and in that heap of living death my bodydrives no longer moved, almost. This present asceticism pleasured me just as much as the biggest orgy, in the memory of man, as they say. And nothing, in heart or in body, it's the same, has begun to bleed, out of pain. The red liquid seen was good as milk, of old.

I write to tell the times and spaces between the nothings, the places between the holes, in-betweens from where one might never return and never talk about. Those times, those places, where pleasuring and suffering are beyond measure, from where, however, language returns without ever being able to absorb them, completely, that's its due, both its beginning and its end. Wanting it to be otherwise prolongs the exile, its distance, its lure, its most certain incommunicability, its formal mastery or its schizophrenia. You showed me absolute oasis syntax and I told this broad breast, our mother of milk, and this thin mouth that never had enough of it, why suffer for it, no one ever did. Talk to me about her and our memory will never be able to support that lexical machine taking her place, between us.

No models for those who are seeking what was never found. Everything is possible, even me, appropriating for myself my most remote strangeness, I would not have wanted any barrier to it. Purple dreams, hoarse raven eyes all round, strident mole, scarlet vultures, webs of my archaic fears, they preached logical metaphor and coherent images to me. I quenched my thirst on their nonsense at the gates of accepted madnesses and absolved murders, scorning my own understandings of defeat, my dizzying reason for being, as if it were necessary to adjust all my senses to muddy language. We are always born the suicides of someone, of some sentence sunk like a nail, rusted in the throat and in the soul, a rope around the neck, like vain hope, hung.

I want the revolution of proletarian housewives workers labouring bodies exploited and won't kill myself if I don't see it come right now. Historical truth, the richest in images, delirious fantasies, multiform characters, multiple splendours, fervours of flaming desires jewels rubies and diamonds, mysterious giants of Easter Island, oysters pearls and salamanders, words of love and body of words. Silvery crystal words.

as if to hold up pursuit longer   never, bedazzle you me and this cyclone clinging kitchen inside I remain   for today   to set my spirits in order   well-being poured on my warm thighs asleep in the morning and I mused on that cartoon strip without words of the night black lines on white of the complicated world that you had the job of deciphering and we would be at peace   he read and commented on everything at once   I swept did the laundry never wanted you to die I swear it   today I'm resting because that yesterday night impels me   suddenly from this film of dream emerged Maria Barzola of Bolivia crushed to death under their boots clubs body rolled up in the banner for a strike sewn with your hands   with your hunger at Cativi in 1942   and me in my village of Amqui then I was learning to talk how much longer did I say so that the wa i ll of our isolation would give way   then when you left your prison Eva Forest I'd walked all day did the shopping made soup for the children and I laughed like them with dammed-up tears flowing free

The way of meaning of this extraordinary luminescent bodily metaphor that I am
When like so many others I almost bruised myself on their censures until the exhaustion of all language and lying in their anticipated psychosis a huge burst of laughter as wide as the universe came from the depths of my bowels and came like a crossrain of happiness the silent night mingling with the rustling of all living things effervescent in their somnolence
Like a positive, happy epileptic fit without anguish each jolt brings well-being in abundance a surplus of intelligence and the way of meaning of this extraordinary luminescent bodily metaphor that I am in its rehearsal

Coenaesthetic images, acoustic images, I understood the rustling of words rubbing between you the fleeting, fragmented shadows of the insideoutside why was that law-woman saying all through the dream and in fact, so often, why tell me, you whom I love honey-woman, the law-woman, mean regulation, with her long finger pointed pleasure forbidden, inside, she repeated endlessly: you have no right to pleasure, to be beautiful, to write beautiful books, to be recognized, loved. To be pleasured. Why this cold relentlessness, and my powerlessness to respond and my silence still shivering with censure and my subsequent delirium and our so long isolation-torment and why the next day did the law-man say, 'You think too much of yourself. You're too much in love with yourself.'

love, rock me still. I don't want to die or turn mad nibbled away by their spoil-sport viperous dissentresses power power millipede fascisms HOWLING
        here lie I from memory forbidden

The old life/lady bawl like a child for the hollow dreams embraced at that age normally they aren't psychoanalysed anymore this whole left body I was looking for oasis words this whole left body mouth full of fingers maledictions marshes this left body I remembered taking her in the arms of my words, putting her into the earth of my tears, closing her up under it, under them, face pressed against their imprint, to never forget that the core of what they tell refers only to the void to the absence to the loss of what cannot be transcribed, ever but from this full, fleeting beginning I was never free. I will choose countries to bring me closer, I will press my ear to the marble of her name, her sonorous fibres will resound in me, she will continue to rush there where I cannot be and I live from it, that flight

so I know from inside and from very far this land without boundaries

A field of wheat. Right in the middle of a thick forest, a field of wheat. She is completely stretched out, inside, a woman, as if asleep, her head on a flat slate where it is written, hieroglyphs. Letters have been engraved of which she understands neither the order nor the meaning. With her index finger, she brushes the wheat dust from the hieroglyphs. She blows on the slate. Meaningful words never learned anywhere emerge. Everyday words.

The anagrammatical plan of fraudulent fiction that attempts to reproduce the unconscious without analytical work and no (unconscious) formulation can ever imitate without (conscious) interpretation the third ear or the floating ear listening as much to symptoms as to lacks. What lure to simulate an outline of mnesic sound already there which cannot be deciphered without constant references to the fables accompanying her plan. The writings clinging to it settle in perhaps in spite of themselves but what matter fences of illusions barricades of exclusions more and still more fortresses of blinding powers.

paragrams mobility of the text scriptural grams moving grams vibrate with fictions programs grams of sugar grams of sex it is the infinity of psychological linguistic codes the infinity of heart luck mallarmé mozart cixous stockhausen haeck straram grams for grammar apprenticeships weave the ordered web from the beginning to the end constraints transgressions or for mobility desire tenderness and all the fashion and modernity together for orgasms no longer have anything on the program neither anguish nor anger nor war nor passion nor tenderness and for desire alone that this distant precise movement that decrypts and deciphers the forsaken inscriptions of graphs and loves

which took one sound for another one word for another one object one face a whole left body with the image inside for another engraved

stone eyes mimed this farce at their own speed

from lair of the dead

She is dead expulsed from forgetting on mauve beaches, left little stains like smoke on my indian ink, without that shadow the first words would never have been produced and there is a tendency not to know that there are no shadows in full darkness in the bellies of our siberias with the barbed wire of our bones with our jailer bodies I surveyed the cold power secret labyrinth and dripped daily words that are suckled and swallowed with the first milk they went back those watch words and it gave me volcanic nausea I saw many quench their thirst on rusty water some tried to escape from those lichens and we are numbed few in numbers, lying in wait flesh-coloured with hate these flipped children whose hearts, they say, she has devoured She   leaves them stabbing   voracious mother not having been able to pleasure in him oral mistress unsated   bites howling bitches

ogresses of splatterings whole nights of insomnia   twist entwined in the narrow nuclear mono bleak beds cramped desires already the twisted fibres of fascism crumbs from their tales stick between my teeth

bysia cava nai y soum kaya isoulava istalinki yani vili grasni VIE i mu drie ka voue ne a kou ni mustava very sou very sou zynio DALOT a

the exit for her exists never MIND your eyes we may never return to you OR we may try a last trip to free YOU* it's a cry from the heart

* Translator's note: English in the original.

alone your vague servitude stretches out skeletal crushed between your feverish fingers that metonymic christ   culpable cosmic curates   sons of castration   erect spit on half-starved children   clinging to them by suction in a chain   ooze from long, dark corridors they call seduction

and phallic mothers lingered like shadows dusty from powders of amniose and lactose   of gold   of larval bloods of bones of hecatombs of choked-back tears of mnemesic sweat from distant orgiastic mailchildren

I know it neither from faith nor from any god   I know it from outside as from inside   from night as from day from previous death as from present life   from conscious inscriptions of a codified history

           from the incipherable unconscious land in fallow

I know it from the numbers of those who accompany me   I know it from the silence of her who has come before me from the well-traced ruts and from those I explore   from the other as from the same and the different   from the linear and the round   from the rectilinear and the complex from the labyrinth and the plain   I know it from my belly dying from lucidity rather than vomited into their visceral tubes   giving myself significance through them   each one wanting a key from this quest   the ultimate question of being until the end frightened of getting lost together looking for ways out   the only question like going there madly pursuit hunger is reborn from its exhaustion obsess me ticktock dragging undertow obese me the effects of her story   from which she was tirelessly disembowelled even skinned alive up to us to reconstruct any reminder murder any reconstruction destroy and from that alone celebration invites us

she said it 'ts' enough I've had it up to here pretty near
squashed under the   wheels of a train that goes full speed
ahead   I got myself out of it   completely new stuck
together earth worm
an' gave herself the right t'think right out loud
an' gave herself the right to right-out-loud thoughts

and besides will be the calm distant smooth thin diaphanous death of me   vaguely remembered   the memory I abandoned forever   no will no bruises pleasuring passion initial recognized sated cry so it seems language will say what from instinct to politics was scratched out but also kept permitted realized language filter strainer will come the time of sharing will come the happiness from the froth of the centuries me I don't want any of your kingdom never pleasured in your tomb neither with your king nor with your princes listen down to the dregs listen to the fibres and the marrow and the heart of pleasure listen no longer possible to wait for tender child of this servitude of father absence and voracious mother bitter sea the cycle begins again exasperated exacerbated light bodies convulse and your rapist sex becomes erect alone and the piles of flesh rusted lines small body bleached by the years where you come from so bruised-bad inverted woman soft and terrible first phantom sterile images subordinate to him the ill-conceived reproductions his story boring unto death when analysis leaves him desperate in their praying sex grammars

my sons are just rebellious, the most beautiful of what I gave them
I do not refuse the story they tell me
but, faced with mine, unheard-of, they keep quiet, dumbfounded by those words yet to come, submissive as if in swaddling clothes, watching for any move I make
Sometimes I concentrate in order to love them better
They have suckled on my revolt, sucked the breast of an old murdered witch, shared in the symposium of the leathery Xanthippe, drunk the pool of milk of a black Ophelia, eaten the juicy orange of my uttermost eden
I rocked them to the rhythm of the mauve tales of my foremothers, in me

Anchored to the ground in the light of the full phosphorescent moon. I am trying to find the lair again, for now. On the amber walls, all the cracks, blind exits, from which the cold sweats of the ambient universe ooze. How in this cove can the hearth be built, where to exit, or else absolutely dispossessed of sounds and images, my mother went to sleep curled up under her bear skin cloak, waiting for the squalls to stop, counting the time of no longer sleeping, of never being able to close eyes nor ears, nor inside mouths nor outside mouths. She is sweating.

Then I hear the wind blow, drawing me from my damp torpor, now a rhythm starts up and I, in turn, watch her anticipation, deprived of any space, but an infinitely long time for those sneaking outside those walls breathing the odour of emerging life. The sudden avalanche, darkness, the water would be solidified, once again. Moon stones of our folded memories, glistening fabric in my words, my meaning in her veins, I was completely unaware of the trajectory of her loss and did not want to force the door of her dreams, strange, swarming objects, cords of suckling babes, talking eels, inflamed serpents hanging onto life clinging to our acrid ochre earth. Grumbling, singing or else quite dumb with fright.

in the coffins of solid bodies the children of their violations convulse backwards orgasms hiccups sobs of their strange eucharistic marriages troubling tales persisting in

$^{bl}_{\ f}$eeding hate taken for love possession taken for passion

she-wolf lovers come down from very far away from a thousand times death from a thousand times life tell you your king is dead crushed between your feverish fingers this metonymic christ this cry comes from the heart of the night unravel unwind as far as the most worn frock linings strip old layers of varnish from the generations from the centuries from the millennia war hatchets to the core to the nerve to the marrow red wood cut and breast swells when the nerve fibres laugh from one mountain to another twist in those new dawns with neither king nor master nor slavechildren

like brothers loosed when the earth was pleasuring

in this desert of rhythmic ogres the sands are deaf and the imagined celestial celebrations far away open my heart they are there
the refusal of those celebrations camouflages for them what wound were they devoured by an ogress mother suckled on choked-back tears fed on whips black tears squeezed among the strata of mute dreams giving drink the knots of the great murmur female universal equivalents in their cannibal commerce and carnivore masses bartered and capitalized loves will all the orgiastic thanatic sadistic pornocratic warrior shamans disappear with them?

and my madness lives within me till I die of it when to cross the shackles of their burning iron divide I touch the keyboard of agony they sow death to all the winds and their words are born sobbing in their throats

writing reconstructs what has been eaten away by the erosion of time, redecorates what has been bleached by the years, never deconstructs any lures, resistance or just dust in the eyes, from head to toe. Dialogic sphinx with her passionate voice, she flies, but always drags behind her the voice of the other woman, the spoil-sport, the doxa.

laid themselves out there in their book coffins, printed their bodies bone by bone pain by pain, vertical sex hung in the engraved stone their immortal enigma

I write to destroy that call for narcissistic mirror amnesia, to devastate what isolates me from the first constitutive images, I am dying from the negation of one or the other of those movements and I love madly what is annihilating them it is written in that tenuous breach lucidity-unreason where madness-dementia has no place, I became translucence, a soft epilepsy in the full light of pleasuring and only had to destroy what I loved destroying me

I will not help with the construction of new-exile lands for our children. No concentration camps, through the levelling of contradictions, no neutralization of images, styles. To conquer the subjugation lying in wait for us, with each cycle, we must identify in each one the precise location where power is loved. Understand that no one escapes that love. Know the urgency with which power from the first breath of life spurs us to survive. Share that grave hope with no illusions. I want writing to draw near its fraud and love itself in spite of everything. I do not want to love the way someone carries a flag. A precise memory of milk of blood has kept me in language, although it surrendered to the most total nonrepresentability

it surrendered felt without experiencing, it surrendered seen without seeing it, as if drunk without drinking it from her who retires before my young strength and I persist in not wanting to empty the heart of words

You lead me into that oasis mauve water of bitterness that they have not been able to talk about. Imagined it stagnant mother, turbid mother, black sea, and troubled by that lack, by the loss of her, they proclaimed childhood symbiotic or the mother phallic. Too many schizophrenogenic mothers so named by sons sick from incest, the ogresses of their white nights, black snow, in their image, inside, were devouring themselves, that ball of forbidden desires while their mothers in the walled-in outside of their own confinements, murdered and raped
do not ask me anymore what is love

break the sound sense barrier

the hysterectomized old woman had written in red ink over her whole body, along the marks and scars, along the ancient complaints: I will be your tireless undertow, your constant return, your eroding wave and never again will you be able to rely on my cycles, I will be your disordered seasons, your unfaithful calendars, your anarchist moons, your out-of-order countries, your centre shores and your trackless tides, your perforated earthly circumference, your diverted current, and never again will you swim there. You will no longer sail. You will be condemned to walk. You will want to irrigate, dig, extend, stretch, take me back to olden days, to the known, to the conventional, you will endlessly collide with that image of me worked by you, you will find nothing there but your fantasy and life for you will at last begin. But I will be long dead to your earth, your grains of sand your coral your canals, I will be dead on your shores, I will be dead mother of your children, when you made a dry crossing of the red mothersea, the sea opened up and in that holy passage they forged an alliance among themselves

in my new lair I remembered that pact

Let me cry, she said. A mother. Let me cry all the tears of my body and of the bodies I rock, let me cry, it does you no harm, and I won't scream anymore. I promise you the tranquillity of that curtain of water that will not keep us from looking at each other, as long as you want. Let me mourn, wrap myself in my pain and regret having borne all those children who have big hearts but still tear each other apart before my eyes. Let me contemplate my unhappiness, steep myself in it, wallow in it, let me get drunk on my tears. Let me sink alive into it if I feel like it. Mad mad mother gone who knows where to the end of my waters. Let me die of loving you anyway. Let me in that death still love you. Let me never want to hate you. Accept my desire not to kill you. Let me weep till the end of the world and so let me rock you tenderly when you can no longer stand your hates and their sharp lines on my whole written body, desolation. Let me comfort you for my unhappiness.

But no one understood this ability to commiserate very well. I even believe it scared us. Strange in her incessant monologue, her inaudible speech.

Will they come as far as inside, the impulsive womb, assume for themselves the inscriptions clinging to it, sticking, oozing, even before I quench my thirst on them, body pearls, double child mother giving birth in her turn, getting happy drunk, in the folds linking what had escaped discourse, many complaints, murmurings, beautiful legends, in the hours of winter when it was rocking itself without seeing, knowing, will they come and tear them down before the epic is unfolded, come to term finally, with no references other than everything that was, in passing, ignored? Could this question still be too young, a residue of archaic fears, from the belly, driven in like needles of misfortune, rag dolls left lying under my bed, laughing nastily at me in my own demise, many, coming from mysterious islands to ceremonies that would lose me, the better to catch me again?

The shaman persisted in breaking up our roads, got the wrong country, thought he was in enemy territory, betrayed all of ours, all of mine, cast aside the frightened little girl on the shoulder of the night road who was dreaming of herself old and him, wanting to smother those fragments of her systematic whole, those patches of ourselves sewn patiently back together, so that they would be emptied of their meanings, cut to shreds, unravelled, while still upon our silence would reign his great book, the solitary testament?

He does not need to say: *I would like to get out of the chain of meaning* for fiction to unfold in its own time on strips of writings, unconscious. She owes him her lack and her strength, the stamp of letters glimmering on the wall of love

She spoke to me of her blood and mine

Once upon a time she was, my mother. She knew all about what left me. Escaped from me, blood. Faced with my death bewitching me in this form that I refuse, why. My mother dead in me teaches me of her labours, of her pains. My words of her that embrace me in my turn. With her pains, with her hours, I tarry. Cling with every fibre to her bruises. Die of she who. Of her stretched out within me. Run along and under my walls. Palpitate and miss-takes us, from milk to blood, from blood to salt to water. When the round uterus is lost, inside mammaries, my memory going, hollowed mother of mine. My precocious death, my graven shadow, that open wound, but closed again. My beautiful beloved, my blessed darling, my half-filled abyss of pain, my love to you. My words awakened, by you, the day you spoke. You took me in your words as you did in you arms. You called me in your vertigo and I recognized your voice from the inside. Through your bleeding cut, I slid. Through your parting of age, in that in-between of yours, in my turn, I spoke.

In that space-place of our bloods, weaned, you had me enter. I knew, through your request, that in-between of mine. It is not possible to talk without lair-between of hers. Knowing from the two of us, the end, through the beginning of cycles, unable to be unable. What around us they named delirium taught me the danger of silence. That vertigo of the in-between-us of our forced weanings. Our bondage of not saying it. Our words fallen from our bellies. Our apparent disorder. Our finally meaningful words. Our red oasis. You were thirty-nine years old on that hospital bed, hysterectomized. In that cold linen, bled white. I was twelve years old, only just menstruating. On the edge of the bed, on the edge of our young old-age, of us both.
I no longer saw you as anything but dead mother of your children.
I saw you adrift from me.
I did not see myself going to your rescue.

In that void, suddenly, that tenuous space, you implored me, to survive. You saw me new with my eggmoon belly and you said 'I want your blood in my veins' and no one else could satisfy you. I knew it from inside your milk of that time. And I said yes to mine of today. They said no to your request. That blood, for them, incestuous. That gesture, in excess, that they kill every time. That censure that we, from then on, could recognize. Their metonymic science. Our glimmerings extinguished. A snare to get caught in. But we knew the strength of our young alliance. From her, I now had a daughter. Words of white water, words of red water, would forever take her, carry her.

She had given me the voice of all our ages.

Last night I dreamed these two sentences:
'Why don't *you* have any children?'
'You see, life is a series of injustices, then we'll see after death'

but there was no punctuation, or at least no one thought of it, and a single character split in two. That is why climbing high on the guard railings of language might give me vertigo and drag me into the watery void very far below

She said, her legs beating on the shores of the void:

on such nights, I warm myself on every word

The field of wheat.

Stretched out in the field of wheat, in the calm space of that dissolution. I made the opposite bet of lot's little girl and of the great indian chief. Without lacan, I would never have seen the great black hole where women did not exist. I come back from the lands of salts and corals. I come back from the valleys and the steaming humus. I reconstitute myself, stick myself back together, under the burning sun, between one storm and the next. Between the night of yesterday and the night of tomorrow. Between the departure of my brother, son of the great chief, and his imminent return. Between two rows of trees, two rows of hate, two rows of love. Down where speech has not yet dared to go. Risking it, will the words go into convulsions, hallucinations? Into inanition?

What does that body of hers say first?
Morphemes, semes, without words. A body that flows, a writing that follows, running away with it, seeping in everywhere the body carries it. Material body engraved with material signs, materials of the gesture that transcribes them faithfully. Hysteria is not amorphous. It is in the oven of meaning. Burnt meaning. Aphonia, in the burning of the sign.
That body of hers says first that she bleeds.

Droplets at the beginning. Then a trickle running along the walls. Soon a stream rushing down the mountain, joining the river, forming a lake, she bathes in it and the whole field of wheat a huge red sea illuminating that corner of the earth lost in the disordered belly. The violence of a history had deposited all its effects there. She would bleed, she felt, and it would never stop. The ardour of meaning. She would bleed death into life, she would bleed hate and lies, cries of possession, desires for conquest, she would bleed love named seduction, and censure named revolution, she would bleed the bruised body of the world and all its children dead of being caught on that flypaper, she would bleed the body of cheated life. The words would flow from her, without phonemes, without noise, if not, from very far, the lapping of her waters caressing the golden sands.

Shore sands that take her back to her centre and keep her from dying. Beach sands where they will come to stretch out, rest themselves, hands on her burning belly, breasts against their sweet mouths, remembering those former times when they were inside. They will love each other under that sun of the Caribbean or the Aegean Sea, as they loved each other in the forests of the Gaspé.

Sands holding her in the fragile coalescence of image and consciousness.

Remembering their mute mothers, the dead mother of each of them, the same and different, who had not been able to give meaning to those signs that linked them to her. Who had not been able to say anything of that so great human carnage all around. Who had disappeared even before her children could symbolize her fate of mute death.

In the red wheat, you see, right in the middle of that flood of meaning, at high flaming noon July, bordered with reassuring shores, laughing, we comfort each other, love, for that initial abandonment, sitting calmly in the hollow of pleasuring.

We have become Bolognian stones. At night, from now on, we will radiate the rays that we absorb during the day.

Coming out of a stone belly giving rhythm to our pulsations, our hieroglyph words will put an end to the illusion of the known, to the mystery of inert slate.

She would have become the very heart of the stone on which her head rested, having consented, having given herself entirely to the perfect trap of memory, not having refused its blanks, having even stuck to it, until the half-light returns, the band contrasting black and white, lines and between-the-lines, inscriptions and margins, was dissolved in the meaningful in-between.

From lair of the living

Exit

I decorated little chocolate eggs, sewed badges on christophe's shirt, carried the african violet and begonia to the best window, on the east side, for them, went out on rachel street between st. lawrence boulevard and lafontaine park, it was raining hard the last snow of the year, the puddles reminded me of all those easter mornings of my childhood when we could finally put on our rubber rafting boots and eat candy, I suddenly felt perfectly happy and heard myself say all day.

A Chronology of Published Books by Madeleine Gagnon

Les Mort-vivants. Montréal: Editions HMH, 1969.
Pour les femmes et tous les autres. Montréal: Editions de l'Aurore, 1974.
Poéltique. Montréal: Les Herbes rouges, 1975.
Amour parallèle, in *Portraits du Voyage* (avec Jean-Marc Piotte et Patrick Straram le Bison ravi). Montréal: Editions de l'Aurore, 1975.
Mon Corps dans l'écriture, in *La venue à l'écriture* (avec Hélène Cixous et Annie Leclerc). Paris: 10 / 18, 1977.
Retailles: complaintes politiques (avec Denise Boucher). Montréal: Editions l'Etincelle, 1977
Antre. Montréal: Les Herbes rouges, 1978.
Lueur. Montréal: VLB Editeur, 1979.
Au Coeur de la lettre. Montréal: VLB Editeur, 1981.
Autographie 1. Fictions. Montréal: VLB Editeur, 1982.
Pensées du poème. Montréal: VLB Editeur, 1983.
La Lettre infinie. Montréal: VLB Editeur, 1984.
Les Fleurs du Catalpa. Montréal: VLB Editeur, 1986.
L'Infante immémoriale. Trois-Rivières: Ecrits des Forges / France: La Table rase, 1986.
Les Samedis fantastiques. Montréal: Les Editions Pauline, 1986.
Au Pays des gouttes (Illustrations de Mireille Lanctôt). Montréal: Les Editions Pauline, 1986.
Femmeros (avec des dessins de Lucie Laporte). Saint-Lambert, Québec: Les Editions du Noroît, 1988.
Toute écriture est amour: Autographie 2. Textes réunis et présentés par Jeanne Maranda et Maïr Verthuy. Montréal: VLB Editeur, 1989.

For a complete list of other writing by Madeleine Gagnon, including translations, see the bibliography in *Toute écriture est amour.*